When Daddy Took Us Camping

Julie Brillhart

Albert Whitman & Company,

Morton Grove, Illinois

Text and illustrations © copyright 1997 by Julie Brillhart.

Published in 1997 by Albert Whitman & Company,

6340 Oakton Street, Morton Grove, Illinois, 60053-2723.

Published simultaneously in Canada by

General Publishing, Limited, Toronto.

Printed in the U.S.A.

10 9 8 7 6 5 4 3 2 1

Library of Congress Cataloging-in-Publication Data

Brillhart, Julie.

When Daddy took us camping /

written and illustrated by Julie Brillhart.

p. cm.

Summary: A brother and sister share an exciting night

camping with their father.

ISBN: 0-8075-8879-2

[1. Camping—Fiction. 2. Father and child—Fiction.

3. Stories in rhyme.]   I. Title.

PZ8.3.B7714Wj 1997

[E]—dc20   96-27302

CIP   AC

The text is set in Vag Rounded Bold.

The illustrations are watercolor and pen-and-ink.

Designed by Scott Piehl.

To Rachel Ann, with special thanks to

Ellen, Ginny, and Lucas.

Daddy took us camping
one fine summer day.
Our daddy said, "We're on the loose!
We're finally on our way!"

We headed off, and in a while
we found our camping site.
A grassy spot beneath a tree
was perfect for the night.

"Okay," said Dad, "let's get to work
before the fun's begun!"
We didn't waste a minute,
and by noontime we were done.

As we set off hiking,
Daddy said, "Surprise!"
We opened up the bag to find
our very own supplies.

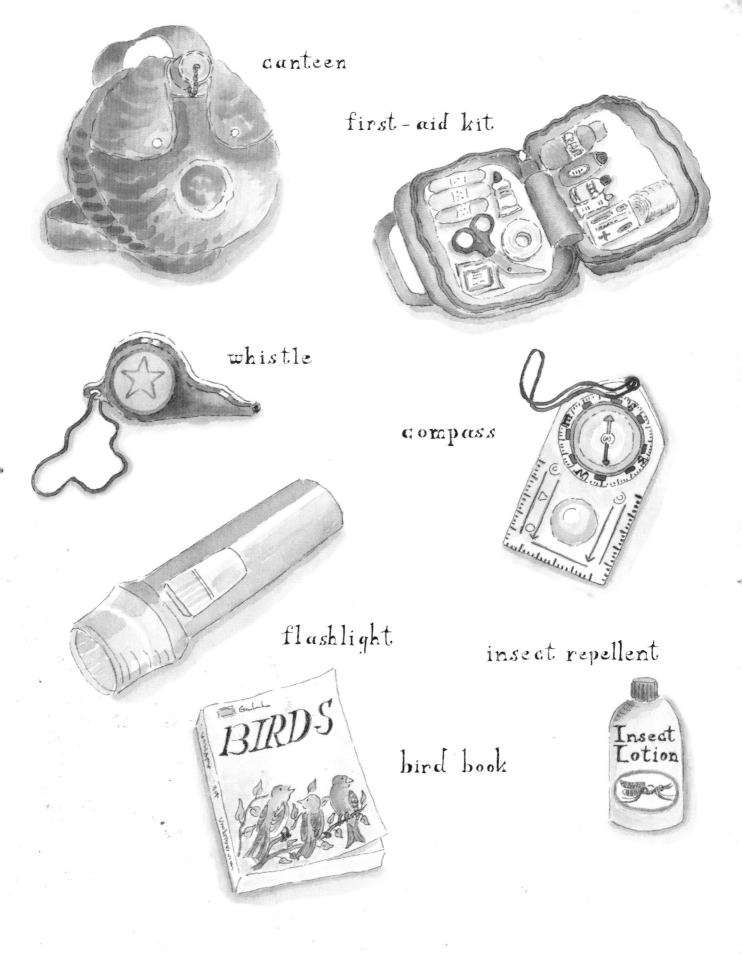

canteen

first-aid kit

whistle

compass

flashlight

insect repellent

bird book

Dad showed us many things
we hadn't seen before,
and taught us how a camper lives
in the great outdoors.

Whoops! We had some trouble
when it was time to eat.
"Not to worry," said our dad.
"We have our favorite treat."

Soon the fireflies came out.
We chased them in the dark.
We caught them in a pickle jar
as they flashed their magic sparks.

When it was time for bed,
we made shadows on the tent.
A monster, bunny, clown, and dog —
then off to sleep we went.

We woke up in the night
'cause we heard a mighty CLUNK.
"Oh no," said Dad. "Is that a bear?"
I said, "It's just a skunk!"

It was very, very late,
and the moon was riding high.
We finally fell to dreaming
in the glow of fireflies.

When morning came, Dad said, "Let's go.
We're hiking back today."
We jumped from bed and headed home—
it wasn't far away!

So if you want adventure
where getting there's not hard,
ask your dad to take you camping,
right in your own backyard!